The world is undergoing rapid changes and if the past few years were of any indication; it's not slowing down anytime soon. It is all too human to resist change, to stay in the comfort zone and avoid the great unknown. However, these things don't last. It's only a matter of time before the passage of time irrevocably changes what's familiar to you; that is certain.

But, inevitable as they might be, changes are not always scary and unwelcomed. In fact, it's an opportunity to challenge the status quo and emerge better than when you began. What this guide seeks to accomplish is to give you the insights and inspiration that you need to best prepare in terms for both opportunities and challenges that's coming your way.

By being conscious and aware of what's happening around you, it will lead you to the outcomes that you want. Even in your most uncertain moments, transition is a certainty. Anticipate what's ahead using tips, symbolism and tools and you will find yourself living an inspired life.

Michele

Cook it Easy
Hello summer

365
EVERYDAY
FENG SHUI TIPS
JOURNAL

365 EVERYDAY FENG SHUI TIPS JOURNAL

Published by Complete Feng Shui
Mb: 0421 116 799,
Email: michele@completefengshui.com
Website: www.completefengshui.com

ISBN: 978-0-6452137-6-8 (Paperback)

Platinum member of the Association of Feng Shui Consultants (AFSC)
Recognised Feng Shui training institution by the (AFSC)

 facebook@completefengshui    instagram@completefengshui

Book Cover, Book Layout & eBook Conversion by manuscript2ebook.com

Welcome to the incredible world of Journaling! Journaling can help in the management of personal adversity and can change and emphasize *important* patterns and growth in life. Writing your thoughts, feelings, and actions down in a journal allows you to connect to your values, emotions, and goals, enabling you to craft and maintain a sense of self.
It can help you reflect on your experiences and discover your authentic self.
Scientifically, journaling can help you:

1. Achieve goals
2. Track progress and growth
3. Gain self-confidence
4. Improve writing and communication skills
5. Reduce stress and anxiety
6. Find inspiration
7. Strengthen memory
8. Add the benefit of everyday Feng Shui tips and watch your life truly evolve…

WHY SO ENTHUSIASTIC ABOUT FENG SHUI...

You may ask what led a young mum of three towards such an obscure field. A roller coaster comes to mind as a perfect description: "Any phenomenon, period, or experience of persistent or violent ups and downs, as one fluctuating between prosperity and recession or elation and despair."

Perth will always be home to me. I was raised by a builder and lived in Belair, Cobar, Bowen, and Echuca. Moving around meant that I experienced many different housing arrangements. I went from prestigious Belair to a home on stilts that rocked at the front with movement.

One home stood out amongst the lot: the home of my Aunty Nikki. Working in a furniture shop in prestigious Subiaco, her home décor was bursting with patterns, fabrics, and textures. I wanted one just like it and aspired to the realm of Interior Design. I studied the profession, which led to architectural drafting. Fascinated by the impact that design elements played within a home, I started analysing my life and the countless houses I had once called home, looking at the shift in life and luck while in each household.

More than twenty years ago, Feng Shui was brought to my attention as it rapidly gained momentum and interest in the west. Like many, I read about the subject. Friends had their homes healed and my curiosity flourished. A Feng Shui consultant came to my home with pen in hand and I followed her around as she instructed on colours, furniture placement and an assortment of symbolism. Red needed to be removed from a wall, furniture directions needed adjustment, Jade and Cumquat plants were to be placed at doors, mirrors, and pictures re-homed, salt went in certain spots, crystals hung to redirect energy. The list went on. The thought of a change in luck stimulated interest and desire. I was in a tailspin – amazed. This was an exciting new venture, a great excuse for an upskill, and unbeknown to me, also a change in my life direction.

I am the Chinese Zodiac animal Rooster, and so I needed to understand WHY I could not have a particular wall red, WHY I needed to place salt and crystals in certain pockets, and WHY was I affected by mirrors or the symbolism of artwork. There were a lot of WHYs, and so my Feng Shui journey started. I began reading any books relating to the topic I could get my hands on. Every wall was painted and furniture textures, colours and placements were altered to follow Feng Shui principles. My home was warm and inviting with lots of energy and light. It looked and felt great. My sister and friends liked the energy and requested I help them achieve similar outcomes. With that, my journey escalated. I began investing in courses under well-recognised Feng Shui masters. I wanted to really understand the many levels and influence of energy that was Feng Shui: the *Art of placement and manipulation of energy*. Feng Shui as an art just clicked; being mathematical, analytical, and practical, it made sense to me.

I loved my hills home, which taught me so much about Feng Shui, energy, and relationships, but it was only the start. Since then, I have successfully navigated the Feng Shui industry for over twenty years, mastering a deep understanding of the multi-layered science of practice.

I have taught Feng Shui, Chinese Astrology and Metaphysical Studies for Silk Road's Asian Studies at Curtin University and worked extensively on interiors, renovations, and with emerging businesses and established enterprises. Through many years of practising and consulting, I became an author and public speaker, and each year, bring my wealth of knowledge and experience to this seminar.

REVIEWS

A must read! Be empowered with these easy tips to enhance your everyday life.
I highly recommend you invest in harnessing the Feng Shui expertise of Michele
Vos Castle to live your best, abundant life and maximise your positive energy to
sustain a happy life and an overall sense of well-being.
Margie Bryant, *Life By Design*

Quiet simply I am amazed. I have done some research on the art of feng shui.
This book was incredibly knowledgeable, practical, very easy to read, and it
appears Michele knows her stuff 10/10.
J T Jewel

My life has positively transformed itself after reading, adjusting and following
Michele's knowledge. I am so deeply grateful and will be recommending this gem
of a book to my clients.
Odette Linton

CONTENTS

WHAT IS FENG SHUI...

Feng Shui means "wind and water." *Wind* is the energy of our breath. *Water* represents how we choose to exist in the flow of our life.

Feng Shui is the ancient art and science of placement, to bring about a balance between people and their environment. It is the study of energy flow through environment and architecture. Feng Shui (pronounced Fung Shway) is a Chinese discipline that seeks to establish harmony and balance in life and the environment. It is an ancient body of knowledge that originated thousands of years ago in China, and it literally means 'wind and water.' Feng Shui is a mathematical, analytical formula-based philosophy taking time dimension into consideration. It reveals how our living space – home, garden office – mirrors our lives. By harnessing the positive aspects of nature, we can create vital new energy.

If we believe the earth is a living thing; everything is alive, everything is interconnected, everything is forever and changing, then Feng Shui affects all.

Traditional Feng Shui combines landforms magnetic influences, eight sectors, Chinese astrology and flying stars.

Today's Feng Shui is similar and practised in many different levels and ways, and with the same goal: to assist in achieving success in all areas of life. Using various methods like landform, eight sector (mansions), Bagua and flying star, all take a systematic approach to addressing problematic areas within a building, home, and environment. Placement, symbolism and tips play a very important role in tricking and manipulating the energy to bring about favourable understanding and outcomes within the home and environment.

We have all experienced Feng Shui in our lives. Many have favourite memories and places; a sense of belonging and security, and harmony within nature and our environment. What you felt was good Feng Shui. The energy of a place, or indeed your own energy, and how the two interact is central to Feng Shui. Feng Shui promises that once you create balance and harmony, you will increase your peace, security, prosperity, happiness, health, love and luck within your living and working environment.

The wonderful thing about Feng Shui is the positive benefit it creates for everyone. Feng Shui is not just about becoming wealthy or achieving success; it is concerned with enriching lives, reducing aggravations, and bringing happiness into relationships. It is about feeling happy, prosperous, and contented. When good Feng Shui energies begin to permeate all areas of life - family, career, health, creativity- you can begin to thrive and prosper

When you know how to be creative in the use of colours, shapes and materials, and know about placement of symbolism and decorative items in your home, you will discover a new energy and zest for life. Life will become joyous; your relationships with loved ones will reach a better level of understanding. Interactions with others will begin to improve.

Feng Shui allows YOU to get to the core issues faster and change the way you live and see life.

Let's start with a revealing exercise.

Before you begin your daily journaling and begin to use Feng Shui in your everyday life, a good place to start is to clarify your intentions.

It is now time to proceed with deliberation and apply yourself with purpose.

Take some time to write out in detail the changes you would like to make.

Change begins to occur from your manifestations and you can see yourself living the new changes – you see them, feel them, taste them.

Feng Shui can help bring about changes in many areas of your life.

- Career
- Fame
- Prosperity
- Relationships
- Family
- Helpful people
- Mentors
- Travel
- Personal growth
- Creativity
- Knowledge
- Education
- Health and well being

Start by writing a statement of intention and commitment on the following page.

Feng Shui, being the art and science of placement, aims to bring about a balance with your environment.

Take a moment to consider all the objects in your home space and environment.

What is it that you see, and how does your environment make you feel?

What is the first thing you see on waking, and how does it make you feel?

What is the last thing you see before leaving your home?

Does it help you start your day well?

What is the first thing you see upon returning home?

How does it make you feel?

At the end of the day, what is the last thing you see before closing your eyes?

How does it make you feel?

Ideally, everything in your space and environment should be special, sacred to you. Do you love and feel inspired by your surroundings?

The first tip of many in Feng Shui is clutter clearing.

I believe that clutter to one may be a treasure to another.

Clutter can cause stagnant energy to accumulate, causing you to feel drained, tired and lethargic. Depending on the Feng Shui area of your home where your clutter is located, it can also negatively influence or completely block the flow of energy in many areas of your life.

How do YOU clear your clutter with Feng Shui?

Firstly, to clear clutter, you need to understand what clutter does to your life. As clutter is a low, stagnant, and confusing energy, it will drain and confuse you.

Begin with focusing on the three most specific areas of your home.

- Your Entrance
- Bedroom
- Kitchen

Consider having a good sort out and clear the clutter. You will improve the energy levels, work levels and productivity will increase no end.

There is also a saying that goes like this:

"To make way for the new to come into your life, you need to get rid of the old."

Increase Money Opportunities!

The first step is Your Home's Front Entrance.

Simple changes to the front entrance of your home can have a big impact on the amount of money that comes in.

Key things to do to increase your money opportunities at the front door:

1. Observe the street or road you live on! The street you live on plays an important role in your home's Feng Shui. Living on a slow-moving, meandering road, gives you a better opportunity of capturing good energy. Good energy is needed to enter your home for positive cash flow.

2. Your cash flow may be hindered if you have a single tree or power pole obstructing your front door. Your front door needs no blockages for good energy to enter.

3. Placing a water feature at the front of your property, with its water flow towards the entry of your home, will activate wealth opportunities, as water in Feng Shui represents money.

4. When looking at trees and plants to use at your home's entrance, the best type is Jade. A Jade tree is a symbolization of money.

5. Your home should always have a clear and clutter-free entrance. Energy comes from footsteps. If there is clutter at your front door and you need to step over objects, this hinders energy flow, which in turn hinders cash flow.

In Feng Shui, there are many symbols that bring good luck and good fortune.

Feng Shui is understanding the flow of chi, the hidden life breath that permeates the environment. When chi is in disarray, misfortunes rule the day. Learn to recognise the hidden energies of chi.

All the energies of your personal space are in a constant state of flux. Yin and Yang energies dance together continually, striving for the cosmic balance that brings harmony. Yin is cool and dark and lifeless. Yang is hot and bright and full of life. Keep these forces in harmony within your home and you will enjoy good luck.

What you see, how you feel and react, gets manifested into reality.
Therefore, symbolic Feng Shui is powerful. Symbolic Feng Shui brings good fortune
to many people. The whole world is symbolic, so if you understand symbolism,
you are on the road to good Feng Shui.

East is representative of the wood element. Enhance with healthy plants,
fresh or silk flowers. Artwork that portrays ideal health. Floral art and patterns;
blue and green colours.

Enhance East to strengthen physical and emotional health.
Improve performance in sports, dance, or exercise cultivate social and
"family of choice" relationships. Heal and enrich relationships with relatives.
Develop inner strength, honesty and forgiveness.

Wooden furniture and décor are best in the East; pillars,
columns, pedestals, and stripes.

Add photos of family members and friends.
Books and quotes on honesty and forgiveness in the East.

Use three stems of lucky bamboo placed in a vase of water
in the East as it symbolises longevity.

The East is the home of the Celestial Green Dragon, so placing a
Green Dragon statue in this section is very auspicious for health.

Place Health Gourd and Quan Yin to further enhance health care
in the East or beside your bed.

Use Yang energy for success. Create Yin and Yang balance with comfortable levels
of light and shade. For success, add brighter lights to enhance Yang energy.

Regular shapes are better and preferred to irregular shapes. Squares and rectangles have better Feng Shui than triangles or shapes with missing corners.

Your main door should be big compared to other doors in the house.
It should be well-lit from outside and inside.

The main door should not face a pillar, staircase,
door, window, toilet or mirror.

The kitchen stove should not be seen
from the main door.

The main door should open into a large bright space,
called a "bright hall."

Never sleep between
two doors.

The front of the house should not be blocked by
any tall building, tree or pole.

The front of the house should be
open and spacious.

The front door should not align with the back door. If it does, slow down
the energy with a mirror, plants or crystal.

Never keep a photo, clock or calendar
above any door.

Your street number or nameplate
should be fixed.

Be mindful of the ratio of windows to doors in all your rooms. Windows should
not exceed 3:1. Too many windows cause all your luck to seep away.
It is also better not to have windows on the wall opposite the door.

Wind chimes work best when placed in the northwest. A six-rod metal
windchime here attracts mentors and influential people into your life.
It also assists the family patriarch's luck.

Display the Three-Legged Money Frog for luck and place it in the
vicinity of your front door, facing inwards as if it has just come into the house.
Don't place the frog facing out the door.

Water features, mini water fountains, and small ponds in your garden
bring exceptional money luck when located in the north of southeast corners.

Beware of straight roads. Don't let the front of your house, especially the front door,
face an oncoming straight road. Block the negative energy coming toward you
with a clump of trees, a fence, a wall, or a hedge.

Ensure that you do not place trees in line with the front entrance, as this will
block your energy flow from coming into the building unless you need to
block the flow if you are located in front of a T-junction.

Curved pathways bring better luck. Any pathway that leads to your
front door should meander, thereby slowing down the chi or cosmic energy
that brings good fortune.

Bring in fresh air. At least once a week, open two windows in two different rooms to
let fresh air sweep away any stale Yin air in your home. It is a good idea to do this
on a sunny day to bring in vibrant Yang energy which attracts better fortune.

Fresh flowers bring Yang energy into your home, but they become depressingly Yin when they wither and die. Never leave dying flowers in your home. Replace them with fresh ones immediately.

Use artificial flowers, which are infinitely preferable to dried flowers. If you have dried plants in your home, your chances of success will be seriously undermined. Never display dried flowers. Feng Shui does not consider them auspicious.

Receive support from behind by tapping into the protective energies of strong
and solid features, such as hills or a large, tall structure, by making certain
they are at the back of your home. When there are trees or higher ground
behind your home, you will enjoy the protection of the celestial turtle.

Water should be on the left. Any water feature in front of the house should be
located on the left of the main door from inside the house looking out. This ensures
the stability of couples living there. Water on the right-hand side is
said to cause husbands to have a roving eye.

The Southeast is the section to activate when you would like a pay rise or an improvement in your finances.

If wet areas, such as a toilet, bathroom or laundry, are in the southeast, you run
the chance of losing money, or having the inability to hold on to your money.
If this is the case, ensure you always close the doors to these rooms.

If you have a stagnant, murky pool or pond in the southeast,
you will have money problems.

The southeast is a great position for a spa or active clean pool. For selling
a property, place wealth symbolism, such as a Buddha in the southeast with
a picture of the intended property and with a sold sticker on it.

The southeast area is represented by the wood element, so use lots of plants
and flowers. As water gives life to wood, use small water features or pictures of
water so you can also activate this section. If using pictures of water, it is
very important that the flow of water is always entering the home.

Never place water (or blue or black) in the bedroom as it can create monetary loss.
You also never place anything symbolic of prosperity in the toilet or bathroom.

The best product symbolism to enhance wealth into your life are
prosperity symbols, such as dragon money tortoise, wealth god, buddha,
gold ingots, or six coins on a red tassel.

Feng Shui teaches you to use your environment wisely. If your land and the surrounding area is undulating, it is said to house auspicious dragons. When land is flat and featureless, the dragon is missing and the land is said to be less auspicious.

Broad contours and undulating inclines are always preferred to excessively steep and craggy slopes. When the elevations are gentle, chi turns benign and prosperous; it moves slowly, accumulating and settling and bringing great good fortune.

The ideal home location is to have a mountain behind, and water in front! In modern landscapes, if there are any tall plants or large buildings near where you live, make sure it is behind your home, not in front. It then simulates the black turtle hills that are behind, offering support. The land at the back must be higher than the land in front.

The area in front of your home and your front door should be left empty, but have a small elevation, or even a rock on the front lawn, to represent the phoenix which is an auspicious feature. It's also auspicious to have water in front.

The land on the left must be higher than the land on the right (looking out from the front door). This is a very vital rule of Feng Shui landscaping.

The Dragon lives on the left of the house and the Tiger lives on the right. You should never allow the Tiger to dominate the Dragon and enter your home, so let the neighbour on your left be slightly higher than the neighbour on your right.

Land is best undulating rather than flat so that it allows the energy to curve and turn. Having land that is flat with only grass is as bad as sharp arrows; the energy moves too fast over the flat field and is not harmonized and meandering. Flat land cannot house Dragons. The more energy curves and turns, the better it is.

The pathway towards your home or in your garden should always be like a meandering stream and not a straight road.

It is good to have the back yard ending up at the gazebo, surrounded by plants and trees. The tall trees offer the support of the mountain behind, and the gazebo can be quite the striking focal point. Also, it provides shade and a place to sit.

If you have a patio at the back of your home, build a small rockery
in simulation of the protective tortoise mountain.

Feng Shui landscaping ideas for the front yard are unlimited. You can have planting beds, a driveway, walkway, or water feature. Your landscape should welcome you with attractive plantings, a nice driveway, and a comfortable walkway.

A curved walkway that connects to your driveway is ideal because the chi (energy) slows down before moving into your home. Everyone loves curved walkways. If you just have one curve, you can add interest by slightly curving the starting or ending points.

A round water fountain in front of the entrance protects you from poison arrows from the neighbourhood. It makes chi, or energy, circulate gently and harmoniously around the fountain before moving into your home. It also represents the Phoenix, which should be in front of the house.

Outdoor steps might be incorporated into a walkway design to raise the land on the left. Create small planting beds along the edges of the steps with low growing perennials

When creating driveways, remember that it should not appear that a straight road is coming towards your home as that brings sharp arrows to your doors, A driveway parallel to the house is not harmful, nor if it is by the side of the house.

Circular driveway design is excellent Feng Shui landscaping. It typically begins at the street, travels across the area close to the front door, and continues out to the street again. If that's not possible, then create a winding driveway.
If your driveway narrows outwards or inwards, it's bad for business and careers. Either regularise it or place lights at the narrow ends.

Driveways that are narrower than the main door, or disproportionately too wide,
are also inauspicious. Driveways should not slope downward, away from the house.
This causes chi to flow outward, thus draining away money and good fortune

Trees will make any garden look special. Their size creates a sense of scale,
while special features, such as flowers, make them very striking. They also
block poison arrows when placed at the sides of an entrance.

A tree standing right in front of your main door
is bad news all the way.

It's best to have tall trees at the back. However, you shouldn't grow trees too near
to the house or they will overwhelm it with their immense growth energy.

Always prune trees so that their growth is controlled. Make sure the trees on the left are taller than the ones on the right.

The stove should be positioned to avoid the cook standing with her/his back to a doorway. A mirror, or any highly reflective kitchen appliance, placed above the stove will counteract this problem by providing a reflection so the cook cannot be taken by surprise. Good lighting and ventilation by the stove will reduce the influence of Sha.

The stove should be at least one metre away from the sink. This energises the stove, making the food that is cooked in it auspicious for the family.

The stove should not face the main door
or any bedroom door.

The stove should not be directly under
an exposed overhead beam.

The stove should not be placed directly
under a toilet on the floor above.

The stove should not directly
face a toilet door.

A toilet next to a kitchen produces Sha; keeping the door closed
and the toilet lid down will help.

Your kitchen should always have sufficient lighting
and be airy and spacious.

Kitchens should never be in the middle of the home.
They are better positioned nearer the back rather than the front.

White is the preferred colour for kitchens. It symbolises purity and
therefore promotes good health from well prepared (pure) food.

Cutlery should not be stored in a stagnant area, as the negative influence of
sharp objects will serve to cut your health. Place them in a drawer
nearest to the doorway or window

To maximise energies from your water feature or pond, use a Golden Dragon
holding a ball facing your water feature or pond.

Place six crystals balls in the centre of the living room
to create harmony in your home.

Place two Fu Dogs for protection at your main door; Male on the right and Female on the left. (You can stand in the doorway looking out to determine left and right.)

For good romance luck, place a pair of Phoenixes
in the bedroom.

Use wish-fulfilling jewels, such as large diamond or cut crystals,
for a boost in earth energy and to request your desires.

Elephants are sacred symbols of fertility
that bring descendants luck.

Two elephant trunks up in the bedroom
bring boy babies.

Two elephant trunks down in the entrance
add protection.

Use images and quotes; from Einstein, fish jumping across the dragon gate, a globe of the world in the Northeast, to enhance knowledge, study and education luck.

To activate recognition, increase wealth
and fame, place a Horse in the south.

NORTH ATLANTIC OCEAN
CAPE VERDE
SOUTH AMERICA
BRAZIL
PERU
BOLIVIA
PARAGUAY
URUGUAY
ARGENTINA
CHILE
COLOMBIA
ECUADOR
SOUTH ATLANTIC OCEAN
Quito
Lima
Cuzco
La Paz
Santa Cruz
Sucre
Asunción
Santiago
Buenos Aires
Montevideo
Concepción
Puerto Montt
Comodoro Rivadavia
São Paulo
Rio de Janeiro
Porto Alegre
Curitiba
Brasília
Goiânia
Santarém
Manaus
Medellín
PANAMA
Virgin Is.
Guadeloupe (Fr.)
BARBADOS
TRINIDAD AND TOBAGO
FRENCH GUIANA
Is Malvinas (Falkland Is.)
(Claimed by Arg & U.K.)
Estr. de Magallanes
South Orkney Is.
Tristan da Cunha Gp.
(U.K.)

Enhance the south for fame, establish a good reputation, gain more respect
and recognition, sustain a high level of integrity

The south section is helpful if you or a family member are up
for an award or entering a competition.

Place a picture of yourself and the award, or what you would like recognition for,
on a red piece of cardboard or in a red picture frame and place in the south sector
with a horse statue or picture of a galloping horse next to it.

Use symbols of accomplishments and goals, photos and images of
respected people, bright lighting. Artwork depicting favourite people and animals.
Items made from animals, such as feathers, bone, leather, and wool.
Triangular or conical objects or patterns to enhance the south.

The south is home to the celestial Red Phoenix, which works on enhancing
your fame, reputation and recognition. Place the symbol of the Red Phoenix in the
south area of your home or work to enhance this for you.

For protection from betrayal, rumours and gossip, place a horse statue
in the south or on your desk or workstation.

Mystic knot brings very good fortune and
endless love if worn as a ring.

Wealth ships carry their vast riches towards you. Fill your ship with money
and sail it into your room from your Wealth direction.

Jumpstart your career with the powerful Dragon Tortoise.
Place in the north.

Mandarin ducks in the southwest
will make your love life blossom and flourish.

Use wind chimes in the northwest to energize your mentor
and helpful people luck.

Broad trees are preferred to thin, spikey leaved trees, except for pines
and bamboo, as they represent longevity.

A single tree in the centre of a yard denotes difficulty and with finances.
Luckily, this is not a common sight.

Five trees in a row in the back garden along the fence line are good Feng Shui,
offering support. If they are fruit trees, they denote the support is also nurturing.
Of course, the trees need to be alive and healthy.

Not surprisingly, dead trees are bad Feng Shui, and even worse if they are
at the front of the house because this is where your energy comes from.

Place orange trees at your entrance
to bring in wealth and prosperity.

Use apple trees for feelings of
peace and harmony.

Red date trees and pomegranate trees
bring pregnancy and recovery luck.

Willow trees tend to bring tears and
a demanding work schedule.

It's a clever idea to plant trees evenly on each side of the house. Trees planted on the left side of a house will control the husband's anger and benefit him, while trees planted on the right side of a house will control the wife's anger and benefit her.

To enhance your popularity, hang either a two- or nine-rod wind chime
(crystal or ceramic) in the southwest. To enhance networking luck,
hang a metal wind chime with six rods in the northwest.

Avoid three in a picture. It is believed in Feng Shui that three people in a picture
can lead to separation unless they are closely related. Three friends in one picture
mean that the one in the middle will be separated from the two on either side.
This taboo does not apply to family portraits.

Where not to hang family portraits in the home - do not hang photographs of family members directly facing the front door, facing a staircase, facing the toilet door, or directly under a toilet on the floor above.

You should never serve coffee or tea in a chipped cup, drinks in a chipped glass, or pour from a jug with a broken rim. Drinking from a cup or glass which has even the tiniest flaw symbolically cuts the mouth or lip, affecting one's speech. Crockery or glass in the home that is chipped or broken should be thrown away immediately.

Always say "no" to the last piece. If you take the last piece of food on the plate,
or the last portion of cake, or clean up left-over morsels at the end of the meal,
you are supposedly creating poverty energies. Resist that last mouthful.

Never sit directly facing open bookshelves that resemble blades, a door or elevator,
a staircase, a long narrow corridor, a toilet door, or the edge of a square pillar.

You should never sit at the corner of a square table with the sharp edge pointed directly at you. If you are eating, you will not have a good meal. If you are playing a card game, you will lose. If you are with someone you want to impress, you will fail to do so. Shift your chair away from the corner.

For Feng Shui for your desk, it's best to leave the part of your desk directly in front of you empty of files and books. Create the equivalent of a bright hall, where good chi can accumulate. Piles of files should be higher to your left than to your right.

Placing items on your desk or within your office space - with a compass, note the direction of each corner of your desk, space, or place. Flowers in the east attract good income luck. A crystal paperweight in the southwest creates harmonious relationships. Place a lamp in the south for good reputation/luck, computer equipment in the west to strengthen your ability to cope under pressure.

Auspicious number eight (8) is widely regarded by the Chinese as a lucky number, partly because the word for eight in Chinese sounds like "growth and development." This number also represents current prosperity, particularly between the years 2004 and 2024. Nine is also lucky since it signifies the fullness of heaven and earth. It is complete and never changing.

Block out excessive sunlight within your office space or you may suffer from too much sunlight and overwhelming Yang energy. Block out excessive light with heavy curtains or blinds, otherwise, the Yang energy will lead to quarrels and a short temper.

What is good Feng Shui for doors? A door should always be solid. Those with glass panels are not recommended. Doors with hinges are preferable to sliding doors. Doors should open inwards to be auspicious.

Energise the Feng Shui of your important files with prosperity coins that symbolize good fortune. Activate these coins by tying them together with red ribbon. It is unnecessary to energise all your files, only the important ones.

A signature is said to attract great prosperity and success if it starts and ends with a firm upward stroke. Develop your own personal prosperity signature and practice it until it becomes second nature.

Here's a secret Feng Shui tip a master gave me, which I have used with
great success. If you have a wish list, write it down on a piece of paper 49 times
and sign your signature below it 49 times. Then burn the paper. Do this
for 49 consecutive days. Your wish list will actualise.

Night energy is excessively Yin, so never hang your washing out to dry after dark.
Your washing will absorb the Yin energies of the night and upset your Feng Shui.
Also, it is not advisable to bathe in water that has absorbed the energies of
the night. It is far better to bathe in Yang water.

Design an auspicious business card for great success. Create your corporate logo with care. Avoid designs that are too abstract or sharp, pointed, or angular, especially if the points are aimed at your name. Use a Dragon as the ultimate success symbol, but do not enclose it so that it cannot grow.

Did you know that seeing a bird denotes Feng Shui symbolism? Birds are a powerful symbol of opportunity. Whether you see the real thing flying in front of you, or hang art depicting birds in your home, they are regarded as lucky symbolisms of good fortune. Below is a list of symbolism for birds:

Birds flying towards you are the best signals, while birds flying away
from you suggests a missed opportunity.

To see a single black bird signifies
an important message.

To see a white bird means healing; if a loved one is ill,
this signifies recovery.

To see a yellow bird suggests wealth or a happy occasion,
such as pregnancy.

To see a blue bird suggests
a promotion at work.

To see a bird with red markings suggests
some sort of honour is coming to you.

To see a bird flying upwards
is a good sign.

To see a pair of birds means
love is coming your way.

To see a family of birds, such as ducks, brings happiness. It denotes the
possibility of a new addition to the family or a family reunion.

Birds building nests in your garden
is a good sign, depicting prosperity.

If birds are singing in the morning,
they will bring good news.

Birds of prey
bring wealth.

Eagles suggest
good fortune.

Sparrows and other small birds are happy messengers;
they denote good news.

Lovebirds suggest romance
or meeting your true love.

Magpies indicate new friends
entering your life.

Crows signify a divine message,
perhaps through a dream.

Owls signify a teacher with great significance
entering your life.

Bird feathers protect from accidents during travel. You can hang a toy bird
with feathers in your car to help protect against accidents.

Birds placed in the South ward off bad business luck. (To do so pertains to the
Bagua School of Feng Shui, which I teach in Module 1.)

Roosters deflect gossip
and lobbying.

The Crimson Phoenix is the ultimate symbol of new opportunities in times of adversity. Displaying the Phoenix inside the home attracts prosperity and abundance. Displaying one hundred Phoenixes would bring one hundred times more good luck.

Get a water feature. Water features are great for improving the wealth of the home or business. Make sure that any water features you have are flowing water. Stagnant water will create stagnant finances.

Make sure you never let the water become green and murky; this will negatively impact your finances. The larger the volume of water, the bigger the impact.

Water features come in many forms. They can be a tabletop or wall water feature, fish tank or bowl, and of course, a fish pond or swimming pool.

Water in Feng Shui represent Prosperity, so make sure that the water is moving and is crystal clear. Also, make sure that the flow of the water is going towards the home, or if it is an inside water feature, into the home. This represents money coming INTO the home.

If you have a fishpond or tank, eight or nine goldfish are the most auspicious amount to have. NEVER have a fighting fish; this creates conflicts. Never place a water feature or the colour blue in a bedroom that is being used for sleeping as it represents financial losses.

One of the best places to locate a water feature is in the southeast section
of the garden, the house, business, or room as this is the Wealth section
according to one school of Feng Shui. If a bathroom or toilet is located here,
do not place anything there.

Have a Money Frog at your front door. The Money Frog is a symbol of prosperity in
Feng Shui and is considered the most powerful of Chinese wealth symbols. Place a
three-legged Money Frog (sometimes known as the Moon Frog) by the front door of
the home or business, and make sure that he is pointing INTO the business or home.

The correct placement of the Money Frog is very important. Place close to the main door, diagonally from the door and always facing INWARDS. This is symbolic of money coming into the home. Also, make sure that the coin (which should be placed in his mouth) has the side with the four Chinese characters facing up. This is the Yang side, which is more active and aggressive, which is what you want when inviting money into your home/business. The Yin side, which is the passive, gentle side, has the two characters on it and should be facing down.

Check out the placement of mirrors. Firstly, look at the front entrance; you should never have mirrors opposite the door. The reason for this is that it shall bounce any good positive chi (energy) straight back out again and isn't given the chance to meander through to the rest of the home/business.

Be careful with mirrors that reflect the bed. For a small child, it may create nightmares. For adults, it creates irritability, lethargy, tiredness and health issues (some may be serious). You can have a solid bed end to block it, or you can cover it with a sheet or tablecloth at night if it is a dressing table mirror.

Avoid large glass robe mirrors. You can either remove or reverse them. If that is not an option, then you can install a curtain to drop down at night. If that also is not an option, then put posters or pictures all over the mirror.

Southwest is representative of love, relationships, partnerships,
receptivity, openness and marriage.

For those having difficulties in their relationship, or would like a commitment
or to find a romantic partner, the southwest is the area to encourage love,
passion and companionship. Enhance the southwest section of your home
or section of your bedroom with love symbolism.

There are many enhancers for activating the southwest. The double happiness symbol can be hung on the wall in the bedroom - it is usually red. Brides in Asia almost always wear something red. It is considered to be auspicious to do so because red is representative of the fire element, so to use this colour activates this section.

Display peonies for love. The peony, "the king of flowers," is a symbol of good fortune associated with women and romance. It is believed the peony keeps love and romance alive. If you have difficulty finding them, a picture will suffice.

For romance and relationship luck to be enhanced, mandarin duck figurines are also beneficial as they symbolise fidelity and happiness. They must always be kept in pairs and sitting side-by-side with their heads facing each other. They are best placed in the southwest corner of your bedroom.

Symbolism that can be used in the bedroom - anything in pairs, e.g., red candles. Heart-shaped objects, happy pictures of a couple. Your wedding pictures, romantic or erotic pictures, sensual figurines, or a sculpture of a man and woman in a loving embrace.

Placing a pair of figurines shows that you are not alone;
you always have a partner in your life.

Never share the wall of a toilet or bathroom or have your head
towards a bathroom or toilet wall.

Your bed should be placed against a solid wall, not under a window.
If under a window, a solid headboard is required.

Never keep any water elements, plants,
or mirrors facing the bed.

A bed should not be kept aligned to the door. Bedroom doors
should not face another bedroom door or bathroom door. This causes
argumentative tendencies with family members.

It's best to get rid of cacti and dried plants. Cacti plants are exceptionally negative
plants to have. Simply speaking, they represent 'poison arrows' and it can affect
health in a major way. Fresh, lush plants and succulents are great Feng Shui;
however, not cacti, even though they have a strong, protective energy.

Having dried flower arrangements are exceptionally negative; they have no life as they are dead! Having them in a master bedroom can create relationship issues and at a front entrance of a business can cause financial challenges

Use Jade plants and cumquats for Abundance. Placing a pair of either jade or cumquats on either side of your front entrance represents "Abundance."

Keep bathroom doors closed. Bathroom and toilet doors should be
kept closed always as open bathroom/toilet doors represent money and
energy going down the drain or the toilet.

Bathroom water should not leak. A bathroom door should not align with the bed or
bedroom door. Do not fix a mirror opposite any door and keep mirrors clean.

Do not overdecorate your toilet or
place products or symbolism within.

Set up your office desk for success. A proper Feng Shui office helps you feel
inspired, productive, and powerful. Make sure that your desk has at least one side
up against a wall. Never have it sitting in the middle of the room. This is what
we call a "Floating Desk" and the result can be that there is no support
for the business or the person who sits there.

Always position your desk so that you can see the doors and windows. You want to make sure that you are sitting in the power position, which means that you can see the door when seated at your desk.

Office positions are very important for good office Feng Shui. Sitting in the power position is a key element. Did you know the person seated farthest from the entrance will have the most power? If you sit too close to the door, you are likely to be distracted by pettiness and daily details. If you sit with your back to the door, you are likely to suffer office politics and backstabbing.

Dining Table Feng Shui - the shape of your dining table is of little or no Feng Shui consequence. The same goes for the material it is made of; glass, wood, or steel makes no difference. This is because the dining table is not one of the three crucial aspects in Feng Shui (namely, the main door, bedroom, and stove) and most people do not spend a lot of time at the dining table.

T-Junction Misconceptions - Facing a T-junction is a definite problem, but the misconception lies with the "remedy." Most people resort to using mirrors to "reflect" away the incoming forceful energy flow. However, as you may already have guessed by now, mirrors do little when it comes to actual Feng Shui. In this case, what you need to do is to ensure that your main door is not directly aligned with the road junction. Use another entrance if necessary. Next, see if you can physically block off the junction view by building a wall, or perhaps with strategic placement of solid trees (or pots of plants) to act as a physical barrier.

Bright Hall Effect - The 'Bright Hall' refers to a broad and open space that allows energy to gather. This applies to playgrounds and gardens in housing areas as well. Houses situated near these open spaces are more "Feng Shui compliant." Next, ensure that the area just outside your main door is spacious and unobstructed (external bright hall). This allows energy to gather outside your property. Finally, ensure that the area directly after your door is also relatively spacious so that energy can enter the property. Note that a bright hall does not involve making it brighter with lights! No amount of bright lights will increase the quality of energy.

Source of Yang Energy - this refers mainly to natural sunlight. All houses should receive a healthy dose of sunlight as sunlight is the natural source of Yang energy. The main door, for example, should be adequately exposed to natural light. Conversely, a main door that is hidden in shadows is inflicted by "Yin Killings," meaning too much Yin energy will be attracted into the house. This often contributes to illness as well as depression. Always remember that "Yang Energy" refers to natural light and not artificial electricity-generated ones.

Colour scheme is often a subject of confusion, even though we all react individually to the variational energy of colour. This is because colour vibrates at different frequencies and creates a reaction in us all. The colour that emanates from your walls has the power to make you feel content, calm, or inspired. Conversely, unsuitable colours make you unsettled, restless, argumentative and can even cause ill health and loss of wealth.

Living at the very top of hills and mountains is not auspicious. On the top of a hill, you will be exposed to strong winds, while lower down the hill and in its gentle embrace, you will be sheltered from the elements.

Meandering water brings money. When water meanders slowly in the direction of
your house, you will prosper effortlessly. Straight, fast-moving rivers carry
water away from you without allowing good fortune to collect.

Waterfalls bring million-dollar opportunities. When there is a view of a
natural waterfall that appears to bring water to your home, you will become rich.
In the Far East, countless people have become millionaires after introducing
an artificial waterfall into their gardens. But remember not to overdo it.
Balance is vital - too much water can drown you!

Protruding corners create "knife edges." Soften the sharp, harmful edges of square pillars or protruding corners by placing a plant directly in front of them. This deflects and dissolves all the killing energy released by the edge. Change the plant regularly since it cannot survive the killing chi coming from the corner.

How can you deflect the killing energy of overhead beams? Exposed overhead beams cause bad energy to press down on anyone sitting or sleeping below. Do not sleep under an exposed beam as this causes sleepless nights and a rift between couples. Camouflage any beams with fake ceilings or hang two bamboo stems tied with red thread. You can hang a five-rod wind chime on the beam to counter this Feng Shui defect in the home or office. Ensure that the rods are hollow rather than solid so that the chi can travel through them and transform into good luck.

Use mirrors to enlarge tight corners. Large mirrors are excellent for enhancing the stale energy of a tight or cramped space. This is especially recommended for tiny halls or foyers. Place the mirror on a wall that does not face the door. Let the mirror create a feeling of space, but do not let it reflect the door directly, since this will cause all the good fortune to disappear.

Trees are an asset. Plants and trees around a home are deemed to be auspicious because the "Wood" element signifies growth and development. They are particularly lucky when allowed to thrive in the east, the southeast and the south. Trees should be pruned regularly and not allowed to overwhelm the house.

Pets are especially good Feng Shui in homes that are left empty during the day. If the family is out working or at school, Yin energy accumulates in the silence and stillness. This can be countered by the lively presence of a dog, a cat, or fish.

Try the turtle exercise. You can do this gentle, calming exercise either sitting or standing with your eyes open or closed. Relax and drop your chin onto your chest. Breathe in, and at the same time, slowly raise your head until you are looking forward. Tilt your head further back until you are looking upward while simultaneously exhaling. Repeat this eight times.

Hang a picture of a sunrise in the south. The south is the place of new opportunities, the location of the Crimson Phoenix. A picture of a sunrise in this corner of your living room will open bright new avenues for growth in your life.

Your sofas and chairs should have generous back support and comfortable armrests.
Arrange them to form a square with a footstool to complete the symbolism of perfect
Feng Shui. Avoid L-shaped arrangements as they are less auspicious.

If you have a fireplace in your living room, the best place for it is on the south wall,
however, it is also auspicious in the east, southeast, southwest and northeast.
The northwest is not a good place for a fireplace. If you have one here,
consider closing it up or simply not using it.

The main door is the "mouth" of the home. Its Feng Shui affects the entire household, so it should be positioned carefully. If possible, ensure that it is not facing a toilet, staircase or mirror, nor facing a pillar, the edge of two walls, or a protruding corner. It should not be below a toilet on the floor above.

Create Feng Shui harmony by painting your front door according to the element of the direction it faces. Red for south, southwest or northeast. Blue for north, east or southeast. White for west, northwest or north. Green for east, southeast or south.

If your toilet door directly faces the main door, install a very bright ceiling light between the two doors and keep it turned on to disperse bad chi and Yin energy.

A toilet in the southwest or centre of the house will affect family relationships. Install a bright light outside the toilet and keep the door always closed.

Toilets should be kept clean and neat but do not decorate them with plants, flowers, paintings or decorative objects. The reverse of what you hope for will happen. Filling the room with good luck symbols causes it to become a symbol of misfortune because its Yin energy is so malignant and inauspicious.

Dining rooms and family rooms should be the focus of a household. Fill them with Yang energy. Paint the walls a bright, happy colour. Keep your stereo system or TV here to create noise and activity.

Hang a photograph or paint a family portrait with every member present.
Make sure everyone looks happy. Hang this in the family room to symbolize a
happy family staying together. Put it on the southwest wall if possible. If not,
it should face the south, southwest or northwest.

If your front door opens straight onto a staircase, negative energy rushes into
the heart of the home. Block this off by placing a plant, a bright light, a wind chime
or a screen between the door and the staircase. Better still, turn the last three steps
of the staircase so they no longer face the front door.

Staircases should curve gently from one floor to the next and be brightly lit to encourage chi to flow upstairs in a slow and meandering fashion. The steps should not have empty spaces between them, since this causes good luck to seep away. Close up the spaces with solid wood to preserve the family's future.

Homes with narrow staircases rarely house wealthy residents. Whether the staircase is straight or winding, if it is narrow, cramped and dark, the flow of energy can get blocked and the area becomes very Yin. Correct this by changing your staircase altogether, or use bright lights and solid balustrades to encourage chi to flow auspiciously upwards. Paint the staircase white and decorate with colourful paintings.

L de MER
Marque Rouge
PARIS
ENCE-ROUSSILLON
KEEP
CALM
AND
SIT AWHILE

Activate the wealth corner of your living room. The Universal Wealth corner is the Southeast. Energize this corner by placing a leafy green plant or a bubbling aquarium there. But do this only in the living room, not in bedrooms, toilets or the dining room.

Enhance your social life with Feng Shui. Hang a bright light and place a cluster of natural quartz crystals in the southwest corner of your home, your living room or bedroom. The light should be turned on for at least three hours each evening. This will transform your social life, but be patient! Feng Shui takes time to work.

How to find a partner? If you are fed up with being single, energize your southwest corner by placing a light there to tap the energy of the earth. Keep the light turned on every evening until you achieve your goal. However, don't use this tip unless you want to find a partner!

Activate romance luck with mandarin ducks. Keep a painting or a pair of ornamental mandarin ducks on a table in the southwest corner of your bedroom to enhance romance and luck. Ducks symbolize fidelity and happiness. An alternative would be anything heart-shaped.

Bedroom Feng Shui. never allow mirrors to reflect the bed.
Reflections in the mirror suggest the presence of a third party.

Just as mirrors are bad news for the bedroom, so are television sets! TV sets create
too much Yang energy and this can cause difficulty when trying to get a good
night's rest. More importantly, having a TV set in the bedroom can create problems
for your relationship. If you do, cover it when not in use.

Good Feng Shui bed positions - always place your bed in the corner of the
bedroom diagonally opposite the entrance. Never sleep with your head
or feet pointing directly at the door.

The door into your bedroom should not face a kitchen or toilet door. Hang a
wind chime between the two doors to dissolve the bad energy created.

Water should be avoided in the bedroom. Displaying paintings of water in the bedroom and blue colour schemes cause emotions and financial losses.

Bedroom doors should not face a staircase, a mirror or another door. If they do, keep them closed or hang a light or wind chime. Do not use a Pa Kua mirror as these should only be used outside the home.

Bed Feng Shui to note - always have a bed head and push the head of your bed against the wall. Sleep at least 18 inches or 45 centimetres above the floor. Never sleep facing away from the door - you should always be able to see the entrance. Keep lighting low and soft. Decorate with dark Yin colours rather than light Yang colours.

Do not hang pictures of fierce animals, abstract subjects or water in the bedroom. Elsewhere, water is very good Feng Shui, but in the bedroom, it suggests financial loss.

Avoid having your bed underneath a window since this will disturb the energies around you all through the night. Use blinds and heavy curtains to cover the window. Try not to sleep directly under a ceiling fan or a very bright light as this also causes the energies to become too active during the night.

When you sleep next to very large windows, or, worse, if the bedroom door is next to the window, the chi entering your room is much too powerful. Your sleep will be disturbed and your energies over-stimulated. The result will be disharmony and discord. Cover the window with heavy drapes, or at least have a second lighter layer of curtains to diffuse the flow of chi.

If your bed is located between the entrance door and the door to the bathroom, the energies that flow across your bed are said to be afflicted. Rearrange your bed or place a screen between the bed and one of the doors.

You may have heard that toilets are bad news wherever they are placed in the home. This is true, but do not fret, since everyone has this problem! Always keep the lid down on your toilets and toilet doors permanently shut.

Beware of three doors in a row. This sort of configuration is a major Feng Shui taboo. If there are three doors in a row and one of them is the front door, the house is said to suffer from afflicted Feng Shui. One solution is to keep the middle door permanently closed. Otherwise, use plants and furniture to create a barrier to slow down the flow of energy, or hang a wind chime between the doors.

Long corridors and cramped spaces - If you have long, narrow corridors or cramped corners in your home, they should be painted white and kept well lit. This ensures that the good energies of the home do not become stagnant and turn into malignant and inauspicious energies that will harm the residents.

Rooms at the end of a long corridor tend to be unlucky. Bedrooms, studies or offices at the end of a long corridor are usually afflicted by killing energies that gather strength as they flow quickly down the narrow space. These energies represent the "classical" poison arrows of Feng Shui. Counteract the effect by painting the door of the room. Red if it faces west or northwest. Blue if it faces south. White if it faces east or southeast. Green if it faces southwest or northeast.

Energize halls and foyers. Wood, Fire, and Water are the elements that create good fortune. "Water" gives life to the "Wood," which develops fruits in the warmth of the "Fire." Keep your hall well-lit and warm in winter. Decorate it with plants and install a water feature - a small fountain or aquarium - for prosperity luck. Do the same thing in the reception areas of business premises.

If you install a water feature with flowing water in a foyer or
reception area to create prosperity luck, make certain that the water
appears to be flowing in rather than out.

West is representative of future, creativity, joy, inspiration, children, family,
and descendent luck.

The west area is representative of protecting family, children,
and of protecting your wealth.

The west does not represent bringing in more money (that is the southeast area).
Rather, it represents protecting the wealth you already have, which is important.

The west is home to the
Celestial White Tiger.

The White Tiger protects
family and children.

The west is also the best area to place pictures
of your family and your children.

For the protection of your wealth, you can use any prosperity symbolism such as
Dragon Money Tortoise, wealth god, and gold ingots.

If the west sector of your home is missed, your family luck and long-term wealth
will be undermined. It is always important to enhance the west.

Home luck, missing corners – Now, every corner has a unique luck residing in it.
You must fill up the missing corners to restore the category of luck residing in the
corner. For example, if the southeast corner of your home is missing, you will find it
difficult to accumulate wealth. If Southwest is missing, then you may never be able
to find a soul mate or satisfying relationship. A missing north corner ensures you
stay unhappy in work and career.

If your home has missing sectors and you have no space constraint, the best way to balance is to build an extension that regularises the overall shape, for instance, transforming an L-shape home into a rectangular-shaped home. The same can be done for U-shaped and N-shaped homes.

If you have a missing sector in your home, you can add a room, patio, deck, or pergola in the missing sector. If this is too expensive, you can simply landscape the corner with plants and stepping stones capped by a tall light in the corner, thereby visually stretching the corner out. Inside the house, you can correct this with mirrors.

Do not build a high wall or a fence too near to the house. This is to allow the auspicious chi to flow around the house. The house shouldn't face anything tall in front of the main door for at least twice the length of the house.

To block a T-junction or straight wall heading towards your home, consider growing a clump of bushy trees; these can be very effective in deflecting all the killing breath introduced by the straight road.

Gates flanked by pillars are excellent Feng Shui landscaping. The size of gates should be proportional to the house. Do not engulf your gate with creepers or vines. Finally, make sure the entrance gates open inwards not outwards.

At the office, always sit with the wall behind you to have the support of your superiors and colleagues. The wall provides security and protection. To strengthen this support, hang a picture of a mountain range behind you.

Do not sit with your back to the door. You are more likely to be cheated and betrayed and to lose in any office politicking.

Do not sit with your back to
a window or bookcase.

If you sit with a window behind you, you will lack support. In any crisis or difficulty, you will be among the first to suffer. Place a solid cabinet behind you to symbolise the mountain. However, do not place a bookshelf there since this signifies knives cutting into your back. Open bookshelves should be closed since they create hostile energies.

The best place to sit in an office is diagonally from the door or facing it.
Desks should not face the door directly, since the incoming energy will be
too powerful. It is a good idea to have a light directly above the door to create
auspicious Yang energy in the office.

Plants in the office are one of the most effective Feng Shui energisers. This is
because they are of the Wood element, signifying growth. Artificial plants are as
effective as the real thing, but dried plants are not encouraged. Place the plants in
the east, southeast or south corners of your office for maximum Feng Shui effect.

Replace defective light bulbs immediately. You should never have too bright a light directly overhead, either in the office or the bedroom, since this may cause health problems. It is a bad omen if a bulb blows in the office or bedroom whilst you are there. If the bulb is replaced immediately, all will be well.

Dressing tables should not face the bed directly. Never position your dressing table directly opposite the foot of your bed. The mirror itself will cause a great deal of bad luck, friction and relationship problems. If you cannot move your dressing table, keep all hand mirrors, make-up and combs inside the drawers and drape a cloth over the mirror. This temporarily solves the problem.

Fire at "Heaven's Gate." The northwest corner of any room or house signifies heaven. Make sure that you do not have a stove or a fireplace in this corner since this signifies fire at heaven's gate. It is regarded as very inauspicious.

Fire and water should not clash in the kitchen. The stove should not be placed next to the sink or refrigerator. This creates a clash between Water and Fire elements, causing disharmony in the lives of the residents. Move the stove (Fire element) to the Fire corner in the south of the kitchen to tap into the natural elements of the directions. Energising the elements in this way brings good fortune to residents.

The Northwest is for enhancing helpful people and travel, meeting mentors, clients, colleagues, and helpful people of all kinds.

Attract opportunities to travel, feel more spiritually connected or bring about a move to a new home or work location by enhancing the northwest.

Northwest is representative of travel, benevolence, synchronicity,
compassion, mentors and helpful people.

If you need to invite a helpful person, or a mentor into your life,
the northwest is the area to activate.

The northwest section can also help
overcome difficulties in selling a home.

Place pictures of people that are influential or inspirational sitting
in the northwest section of your home and office.

If the man of the house is having difficulties, it will benefit him greatly
to enhance the northwest area.

Enhance Northwest by placing metal symbolism in this sector. The best Feng Shui products to use in this area are the three-star gods (also known as Fuk, Luk and Suk). They represent health, wealth, and longevity. They like to be placed waist-high if possible, not on the floor and not directly facing the main door if facing outside. Additionally, do not display them under beams or facing a toilet.

Photos of people who are especially helpful to you - Favourite religious and spiritual figures, objects that carry blessings and spiritual importance, images of special and sacred places. White, grey, and black. Books and quotes on synchronicity and miracles are all helpful when placed in Northwest.

Keep nine goldfish for luck. A great way to activate excellent Feng Shui luck inside the home is to keep nine goldfish in an aquarium; eight red or golden and one black. If any of your fish die, do not worry, just replace them. It is said that if a fish dies, it has absorbed the misfortune meant for a resident.

Display peonies for love, the peony is the "King of Flowers" and is a symbol of good fortune associated with women and romance. Legend tells of Yang Kuei Fei, reputedly the most beautiful woman in Chinese history and concubine to the Emperor. She kept him enthralled throughout her life, and in homage to her, he kept her bed-chamber filled with peonies. It is believed that the peony keeps romance and love alive.

Grow oranges or limes, bright red oranges signify gold because "Kum," the Chinese word for oranges, also means gold. An orange or lime tree weighed down heavily with ripening fruit, thereby symbolising the ripening of good fortune and prosperity. Display them at the entrances to your home.

Hang coins and bells on your doors. Use three Chinese coins (round with a square hole in the centre) tied with red thread on the inside door handles of your main doors. The red thread activates the essence of good fortune symbolised by the coins. On the outside, hang bells, also tied with red thread.
Never hang the bells or coins on the back door.

Avoid having prickly cactus plants inside the home. The thorns of these plants represent tiny arrows that cause killing energies to accumulate. Cacti can be placed outside the home for protection, but bonsai plants, which represent artificially stunted growth, should not be displayed either inside or outside the home.

It is best to place stereo equipment on the west wall. All stereo and hi-fi equipment brings extra luck to the house when placed on the west wall of the living room. Stereo sets placed here create the potential for good fortune since 2004.

Mops and brooms are associated with sweeping out the negative and stale energy of the home, but they can also sweep away good energy. Feng Shui advises that you hide them away after you have finished cleaning, keeping them out of sight.

Always keep things in pairs if you want someone to share your life with.
Surround your personal space with objects and ornaments in pairs,
such as ducks, butterflies or birds.

Decorate the bedroom in red during the early years of a relationship. If red is too
strong, use pink or peach. Red represents passion and strong Yang energy and
brings luck to those wanting children. Otherwise, use more muted Yin colours.

Curved pathways bring better luck. Any pathway that leads to your front door should meander, thereby slowing down the chi or cosmic energy that brings good fortune.

Never put plants or flowers in the bedroom, however, fruit is excellent, especially the pomegranate, which is a symbol of fertility.

Hang paintings of children in the west to symbolize descendants' luck.

Avoid anything that suggests water in the bedroom.

Invite the gods of wealth into your home. The Chinese have several gods of wealth which they display in their homes to attract prosperity luck. You could use Kuan Kung or the three-star gods, Fuk, Luk and Sau, all of whom bring wealth and prosperity.

Spiral staircases are often designers' favourites, but they are inauspicious in Feng Shui terms, particularly when located in the centre of the home. The spaces in between the steps cause money to drain away and the circular corkscrew shape unbalances the house. Spirals in the corner of a room are less harmful.

Square, structural pillars directly facing an entrance should be covered with mirrors or other reflective material, or softened with creeping plants. Round pillars are less harmful, particularly if they frame the front door. However, if they do face the front door, they may cause similar problems.

Screens are excellent Feng Shui remedies as well as making superb room dividers. Screens solve a multitude of Feng Shui problems associated with fast-moving, killing breath. Screens block, dissolve and dissipate bad energy (shar chi), but they must be placed in a straight line, either suspended from the ceiling or firmly attached to the ground. If placed in a zigzag fashion, shar chi will accumulate.

Use colour to create auspicious combinations. Red and orange for the south. Black and blue for the north. Green and brown in the east. White and grey for the west. Light green for southeast. Yellow and beige in the southwest and northeast, and white, silver and gold for northwest.

....

....

....

....

....

....

....

....

....

....

....

....

....

....

....

....

....

....

When corners representing wealth (southeast), relationships (southwest) or health (west) are missing, you will suffer acutely in these areas of your life. You can fill the missing corner by using a wall mirror to visually extend one wall, building an extension or installing a bright light.

If in business, take care when locating your company signboard. Your corporate signboard must always be protected from bad Feng Shui. Place it high on your business premises and watch out for elevated highways and flyovers, communication masts and electricity pylons, elevated railway lines and the sharp edges of nearby buildings.

Earth energy brings excellent Feng Shui. If you want your business to benefit from earth energy, activate the three earth areas of your premises - the centre, southwest and northeast corners. Place large ceramic or pottery urns or crystal clusters in these places. Earth energy is strongest in the southwest corner.

Use mother of pearl for all your wood corners. Enhance the energies of your wood element corners - the east and southeast - with mother of pearl to increase your turnover. The Chinese make mother of pearl furniture for this purpose.

Trim your plants and trees regularly, at least once every three weeks. Overgrown plants that look straggly and uncontrolled are not good Feng Shui. More importantly, you should trim your trees at least once a year. Always make certain that your trees do not overwhelm your home.

Be wary of plants with thorns. Move all plants that have prickly thorns away from the vicinity of your front door. Thorny plants can create a protective energy, but they should always be outside and not too near the front door.

Throw out dried leaves and plants. Dried, wilting or rotting plants emit large doses of Yin energy, with negative results. Stale. water faded flowers and any dried flowers should be removed from the house. Be careful to do the same in the garden. This will maintain the presence of healthy Yang energy.

A door flanked by water spells tears - when introducing a water feature into your home, be careful. Too much water can spell danger. Never have water features (ponds, pools, fountains) on both sides of the front door.

North is representative of self, career, work, success, mission and life's journey.

If you would like a career change, if business is slow, or you are going for a job interview, north is the best area to activate. The north is home to the Celestial Black Tortoise and therefore the Black Tortoise should always be placed in the north to give you career support.

If you wish to activate change, further business and career luck, place a metal object in the north section of the house or room because metal gives life to water.

Add a Golden Dragon Money Tortoise and Prosperity Buddha in the north to further career and business luck.

Develop sensitivity to your surroundings. Good Feng Shui practice requires the ability to spot secret poison arrows in the surrounding environment These arrows hurt you only when they are pointed directly at your front door.

Deflect the created killing energies with a Bagua mirror. Hang this protective Yin symbol outside the house above the front door. Obvious poison arrows are a straight road, a triangular roofline, a high wall, a large pillar, a telephone pole, a tree trunk, or the sharp corner of a building.

Make your main door auspicious by incorporating a small water feature - an aquarium is best, either on the left side of the door as you look out, or directly facing it. Otherwise, hang a bright light above the door - crystal if you can afford it - to welcome in the chi.

Feng Shui energisers for staircases - Always keep the staircase and landing well-lit to encourage the flow of chi. Hang a lucky painting on the landing or some auspicious calligraphy. If the staircase is too narrow, hang a large mirror to widen it.

Have at least one wall without windows in your living room. This wall should ideally face the door into the room. This allows the chi to flow into and around the room instead of escaping through any windows directly opposite the door. In designing floor layouts, remember to let the chi move gently and slowly from one room to the next.

Clear your space with loud noise. In China, the lunar New Year was celebrated loudly with drums, cymbals and firecrackers to wash out old energies and welcome in the new. You can do the same with loud, happy music. Play it for ten minutes - that's enough.

Make a wealth vase and keep it hidden in your cupboard. It can be made of gold, crystal, or glass. Fill it with semiprecious stone and with soil taken from a rich man's garden.

Earth energy is associated with romance.

Placing crystals near you is conducive to energising your love potential, especially in the southwest sector.

The Southwest is an Earth sector, which means the presence of Fire energy will strengthen the Southwest.

Understanding the five elements is the key to unlocking many of Feng Shui's secrets.

When Fire is present, the impact is the creation of Earth.

Place Earth symbols in the southwest corner to support women's luck. You can use natural or man-made crystals, items of porcelain or even semi-precious gemstones.

Make use of the colour red in the home in the South and Southwest.

Red always attracts romance luck.

Place a red lamp in the Southwest to attract romance luck.

Activate the Northwest with metal wind chimes for helpful people luck.

Create a vision board of your ideal partner and place it in the Southwest or Northwest.

Men should hang their love vision board in the Southwest.

Women should hang their love vision board in the Northwest.

For best relationship luck, men should sleep on the left side, women on the right side of the bed.

Ladies, you should always stand on the right side of your man. This prevents another woman from taking your position in his life!

When taking couple photos, for everyday fun, wedding, anniversaries, or family photographs, men should always be on the left and women on the right.

A bed against a solid wall gives you strong backing
in everyday aspects of life.

Never have a floating bed. Your bed should always have the
backing of at least one solid wall.

Never have mirrors in the bedroom as they attract third parties. Third parties don't
always come in the guise of a side relationship - it could also be a meddling in-law,
an intrusive friend, or a family member that gets in the way of a relationship.

To enhance fertility luck, place the image of an elephant
by your bedside with its trunk down.

For fertility luck magic, place a white cowrie shell without any blemishes or spots in
a five-coloured silk pouch and place the pouch under the pillow as you sleep.

The best Earth enhancers for the South are red crystal balls. Place in the South,
to strengthen fame, reputation and love luck.

If your bedroom is in the North, crystal balls that are blue, or natural stone that is blue (like lapis lazuli) are marvellous for energizing your love life.

If relationship luck is elusive, try energizing your peach blossom luck. The Rat is the peach blossom sign of the Rabbit, Sheep and Boar. The Rabbit is the peach blossom sign of the Horse, Dog and Tiger. The Horse is the peach blossom sign of the Snake, Rooster and Ox. The Rooster is the peach blossom sign of the Rat, Dragon and Monkey. Rabbit brings love for the Dog, Tiger & Horse

When you want to activate your Peach Blossom luck, it is a good idea to incorporate the placement of love symbols in your Peach Blossom corner,

Display Dragon and Phoenix
for relationship longevity.

Display Mandarin ducks
for Everlasting Love.

Use one hundred birds
for auspicious luck.

Northeast is representative of wisdom, knowledge, self-improvement,
spiritual growth and education.

Northeast is an important section to activate for anyone who is studying or
doing exams wanting to tap into extra knowledge or spirituality.

The best way to activate the Northeast is by placing a crystal globe or a normal world globe on a table or shelf in the northeast section of your room or house.

Crystal is representative of the earth and is the strongest form of energy for the earth element, which in turn represents the northeast section.

Enhance Northeast with study materials, pictures of quiet places,
such as mountains or meditation gardens. Images of wise and
accomplished people. Black, blues, and greens.

Books, magazines, maps and pictures of the world for knowledge and
self-cultivation, are to be placed in the Northeast.

Display a flock of one hundred birds in the south of your bedroom
or living space to trigger recognition and fame luck!

Phoenix or peacocks symbolize wish-fulling luck
and advancement of status.

Lovebirds invite opportunities of love to enter your life!
Display them in the southwest corner to bring romance luck.

"Dress for success" dark colours like blacks and browns create an aura of masculinity for men. They help you come across confident, authoritative and commanding, traits that females find very appealing!

Ladies, red cheeks
attract admirers.

Ladies keep your hair long to hook a man! Men are naturally drawn towards
Yin energy as this completes the balance between Yin and Yang!

Long and straight hair is the
ultimate Yin / feminine hairstyle.

Allow your hair to grow past your shoulders, and if you wish, add some streaks
of red to channel the luck of the Love Goddess!

Flowers accentuate your feminine charm. Borrow the luck of red flowers by
wearing dresses decorated with red floral prints to enhance your attraction.

Throw out photos of past relationships
that stir up painful memories.

Select an auspicious date
to get married.

Avoid exchanging vows at sunset. While this may seem exotic and romantic, it is unfortunately terribly inauspicious! How can a wedding be auspicious when it takes place in the hours of the evening when the sun is about to fade away?

If you are single, carry your quartz crystal with you when going on a date. Whenever you feel your relationship luck getting weak, recharge these crystals with sunlight and hold them close to your heart. Draw strength from them and you will start to feel stronger and more positive again!

In Feng Shui, size really does matter! If you want greater family luck filled with abundance, prosperity and happy moments, then try to sleep on a large bed! The larger the size of your bed, the more auspicious it is for your family luck.

Place an Amethyst geode with a long piece of red thread tied around it
under your bed to keep your spouse faithful.

Blue coloured sheets and curtains
cause marriage woes.

The bathroom is a taboo place for photographs! Avoid hanging photographs of your relationship and your family inside the bathroom or toilet. Also, be mindful not to place photographs facing the door of the toilet or bathroom.

Never place family photographs at the foot of your bed. When displaying photographs of you and your spouse, or family portraits, never display them at the foot of your bed! This has the effect of "kicking" your family each time you sleep!

Hang a beautiful "togetherness" portrait. The secret to keeping your family unit close and supportive of each other is to hang a large portrait prominently in your living room, letting it take a dominant stage for all to see!

Use plants in your home they are
superb Chi boosters.

The Dragon and Phoenix couple image represents the Emperor and
Empress (husband and wife), which symbolises happy marriage with a lot of
wealth and brings luxury in life.

A peach tree symbolises longevity in Chinese tradition. Displaying a
peach tree image or peach flowers in the southwest corner of your bedroom
can bring great love opportunities.

Placing live pink colour flowers in the southeast corner of your house is believed to bring a lot of new relationship opportunities. Placing a lot of plants in the southeast corner can also achieve this.

The Double Happiness Symbol is an excellent Feng Shui symbol for wedding luck. Its meaning in Chinese is "joy and happiness" and it is written twice. If you wish to find romance and a future partner, it is great to place this symbol in the southwest corner of your house or bedroom or carry it in your handbag or purse.

Natural Crystal Quartz is extremely effective to activate Earth energy of the
southwest corner and it will attract romance into your life, especially when
you place a crystal (or hang it) by the window which catches sunlight.
It will expand Yang energy around the space.

BEGINNERS FENG SHUI
'EASY TIPS TO ENHANCE
EVERYDAY LIVING'

A beginner's guide to learning the fundamentals of Feng Shui and energy flow in the home, known as Chi. This ancient art of placement which brings balance, helps to improve the harmony and prosperity within your space. Ideal as a gift for the novice wanting to learn more or beautiful coffee table book to inspire you on your next home renovation.

Buy Beginners Feng Shui   **www.completefengshui.com**

Ebook Beginners Feng Shui   **www.completefengshui.com**

COMPLETE FENG SHUI NEWS IS FOR YOU - TO NAVIGATE AND UNDERSTAND YOURSELF AND ENVIRONMENT:

Monthly Subscription

- Monthly Feng Shui and Flying Star Outlook
- All 12 Animals Chinese Horoscope Forecasts and Day Masters
- Calendar Auspicious date selection… And much, much more
- Over 40 pages to navigate monthly Feng Shui Subscribe
  www.completefengshui.com

COURSES / WORKSHOPS in person and online

- Complete Lifestyle Retreat
- Understanding Feng Shui and your home
- Landform and Symbolism… making the most of your home and interior Show Me the Money - Chinese Astrology for Career, Wealth and Success Lifestyle Feng Shui - Better Living with Feng Shui
- Good Feng Shui… Property and Real Estate
- Getting to Know YOU, Beginners Chinese Astrology Part 1 & 2
- Module 1: Health, Wealth & Prosperity
- Module 2: Four Pillars of Destiny Part 1 & 2
- Module 3: Flying Stars Part 1 & 2
- Module 4: Practitioners Course and Business Practices for a Feng Shui Business Feng Shui Refresher workshop

TESTIMONALS

I have been following Michelle's Feng Shui advice for over 12 years She is an amazing, very professional person with many of her predications being very accurate. **Dot O'Sullivan**

"Michele has a wealth of knowledge of all aspects of feng shui, which she shares with generosity and clarity. She interprets the Chinese astrology charts of each member of the household with great insight and intuitive understanding. Michele is always empathetic to the needs and circumstances of her clients and has helped me and my family tremendously over the many years we have made use of her services. I highly recommend Michele and her work!" **Annie Vorster**

Michele is a True Master of Feng Shui. I have had her involved with my own homes and my workplace's for about 16 or 17 years now.

She is a pleasure to work with and knows so much about Feng Shui, and how to remedy all situations.
Having Feng Shui in my life has helped the energy of my family and workplace, and make them amazing places to want to be, you can feel the calmness and the energy flowing. I am hooked, I love the beginning of every new year, so see what is changed, I love the Bazi Charts you get too, So many interesting things about life and yourself. **Ann Meney**

Great experience with Michele. Very approachable, polite, and friendly. Michele has a lot of Feng Shui knowledge. I feel that I can still ask her questions even after she has completed my consultation and report. Will continue with Michele for all future Feng Shui and interior design matters. **Mary Valentina**

We have been knowing Michele for over 12 years. Always very happy with the Feng Shui readings she does for us yearly, we often refer to and use as guidance throughout each year.

Michele has helped us with the purchase of our homes.

Happily, highly recommended Michele when you need a Feng Shui master for your house, office, and guidance yearly to get you through the year, year after year fan. Michele is very warm, approachable and brings a beautiful energy within her presents. **Aria & Michael Van Uffelen**

Michele Castle is an amazing Fengshui master and has done a very detailed informative book for my home and family. The detailed charts and reports gave us great insight, her amazing experience and explanations help guide us with what the energy is bringing with the year and elements. It has helped us be best prepared, even for the best Feng Shui for our business and money as well.

I am grateful for Michelle's guidance, and I trust her and highly recommend her to my family and friends for her in-depth Feng Shui knowledge. **Bass Tadros**

I have been fortunate enough to have been introduced to Michele and Feng Shui at least 6 years ago. It came about around the trials and tribulations I was having with the building and surroundings I lived and continue to live in. Well, I took on the recommendation to have her check the place out and was pleasantly surprised at her findings and cures and hence allowing peace and harmony to return to my home again. I have completed some courses with Michele and am amazed at how knowledgeable, intuitive, and magical she is... brilliant Feng shui master in my books. I continue to use her for annual assessment of energy flows etc for my home and other aspects of my life.

Love her work and her as a professional being that she is. I highly recommend Michele as a Feng Shui expert and teacher. **Bhavna Mistry**

Since I first met Michele from Complete Feng Shui eight years ago, she has guided me on energetically restoring my house's virtues, found me a landscape artist to design the Garden of Eden of my dreams and sailed me onto the sweet shores of fulfilling romance. She is my go-to Guru and a master of her craft. **Monica wood**

Michelle is always helpful and willing to advise what works best for everyone in our household. We have engaged her service for over 10 years now on property purchase and annual readings. She is always friendly and so easy to work with. Highly recommend her service. **Frank Walsh**

ABOUT THE AUTHOR

Michele Castle has been a Feng Shui practitioner - consultant for more 2 decades. Trained by Master Raymond Lo, of Hong Kong at the Feng Shui Centre in Perth, Western Australia she has also studied with Dato Joey Yap and Lillian Too. Michele studies each year under various master's and is continually expanding her Feng Shui knowledge.

Michele taught Feng Shui, Chinese Astrology and Metaphysical studies for Asian studies unit at Curtin University.

Previously studying architectural drafting and interior design and working with interiors and renovations, on her own homes it was a natural progression to incorporate Feng Shui and metaphysical studies in her renovations. Applauded for her style, she was asked if she could do what she had been doing with her own homes to others. So, having a passion and dedication after further studies her first Feng Shui business, *Energise Life Feng Shui*, began, growing quickly and incorporating workshops, seminars and teaching it soon became known as *Complete Feng Shui*.

Michele conducts on-site Feng Shui consultations for residential and corporate clients, and as well as being an accredited teacher of Feng Shui, Michele is an author and public speaker. Michele works with residential homes, small to medium family businesses, larger corporations, developers, architects, interior designers, real estate agents, restaurants, cafes, day spas and retail stores. Michele specialises in one-on-one Chinese astrology and life path readings regarding health, love, and career opportunities.

For a business client, Michele can help with staff recruitment, assist with selecting the best location and orientation for business premises, improve the atmosphere and working environments and advise on business stationery such as letterheads and business cards.

For the residential client, Michele advises on how to improve health and harmony in the home, how to choose the best home as well as improve the chances of selling your present home, assist with identifying strengths in choosing suitable careers for the younger members of the family, guide older family members looking for a change in their current career path and how to alleviate difficulties children may be having with sleeping, studying and behaviour in general.

Michele is often in demand for speaking at events, local radio, interviewed on *Today Tonight*, *Better Life TV*, and is a regular on the WA television show *The Couch*, where she talks about all things Feng Shui. Michele has been recognised with local awards a winner of a Nifnex Influential 100 Awards, the New Emerging Business Award, Entrepreneur Award as well as Networking Award from the Soulful Awards Self Discovery Network on 2 occasions.

Michele teaches Feng Shui courses and workshops from beginners to practitioners alike, as well offering Feng Shui Retreats in Bali and now in WA where you can immerse yourself in 5 days of Feng Shui and Chinese Astrology; one of the world's most ancient arts and science of placement, to bring about balance between people and their environment. Michele also conducts on-site learning exercises at homes and for businesses, within Australia and overseas.

For those who have mastered the basics of Feng Shui and wish to continue their studies and share their knowledge with others, there are courses in 'Feng Shui as a Business', and the 'practitioners' course' where with practice and the correct training, one can learn to be a practitioner once mastering Feng Shui becoming a consultant. Once qualified, you have a responsibility to share the correct knowledge with your client. Choosing a Feng Shui consultant is like choosing a health care professional; you want someone who knows what they are doing, who understands your needs, and gives a reliable, knowledgeable advice.

Michele truly believes.
" Life is what our thoughts environment and energy make it".
"Change your environment and thoughts, change your life".

With the knowledge of Feng Shui, it can work to increase wealth, enhance health, and harmonise relationships.

9 780645 213768